THE DOMINIE WORLD OF
OCEAN LIFE

ANTARCTICA

Penguins

WRITTEN & PHOTOGRAPHED
BY KIM WESTERSKOV, Ph.D.

DOMINIE PRESS
Pearson Learning Group

1

Introducing Penguins

Many people like penguins. Why is it so easy to like them? Maybe it's because they seem so much like us. Although they are birds of the sea, they walk, or waddle, like a toddler, and stand upright on land as we do. The black backs and white fronts of the Antarctic penguins make them look like little men dressed up in tuxedos.

▲ *The small emperor penguin colony at Cape Crozier on Ross Island is the southernmost penguin colony in the world. Each autumn, the colony assembles on the new sea ice next to the ice cliffs of the Ross Ice Shelf, or in large cracks or canyons on the ice shelf.*

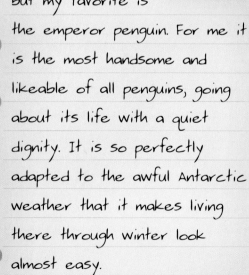

NOTES

I like all penguins, but my favorite is the emperor penguin. For me it is the most handsome and likeable of all penguins, going about its life with a quiet dignity. It is so perfectly adapted to the awful Antarctic weather that it makes living there through winter look almost easy.

These emperor penguin parents are guarding their chicks at Cape Crozier. Emperor parents often stand close together, allowing their chicks to "socialize" with other chicks.

2

What Is a Penguin?

A penguin is a type of bird that has traded the ability to fly in the air for the ability to "fly" through the water.

All penguins have the same basic color pattern: dark in the back with white in the front. At sea this acts as **camouflage**. A **predator**, such as a leopard seal, looks down and sees the penguin as a dark shape that blends into the dark background of the deep sea. A predator that looks up from below sees a vague, light shape that blends into a light background, the water's surface.

Penguins may not look much like birds, but they are, indeed, birds that have become highly specialized for life in the sea. Like

4

all birds, they are warm-blooded, lay eggs, and have feathers, beaks, and even wings. These wings have become short, stiff flippers, which beat powerfully up and down, **propelling** their **streamlined** bodies smoothly through the water. Their tail and feet combine to form a rudder that enables them to steer.

Penguins are found only in the **southern hemisphere**, from **Antarctica** to the Galapagos Islands, at the **equator**. Most penguins live in the cold southern oceans, breeding on remote islands and along the coastlines of Australia, Africa, South America, and Antarctica. Most **species** stay close to home.

The keys to the penguin's ability to live in cold water are feathers and fat. Their waterproof feathers are short, stiff, and tightly packed. The outer part of each feather is

NOTES

Why do penguins walk the way they do? Their short legs are set far back on their bodies, so when they walk, they do so upright with a "penguin waddle."

5

waterproof, while the inner part is fluffy down. This down layer traps air and provides over ¾ of a penguin's **insulation**—this is amazing, as the layer of feathers is less than ½ inch thick. The rest of the insulation comes from a layer of fat under the skin.

Most penguins feed near the surface, so dives are usually both short and shallow.

For penguins, the sea is home. All of their food lives in the sea, and they are superbly designed for life there. Some species spend over ¾ of their lives at sea for several months at a time, coming ashore only to lay eggs, raise chicks, and **molt**.

Scientists have argued for years about how many penguin species there are. Most agree on seventeen, but others say that there are between sixteen and twenty.

▼ *Adèlie penguins*

▲ *Plunging Adèlie penguins head out on another feeding trip to bring back food, stored in their stomachs, for their ever-hungry chicks*

Antarctic Penguins

Of all the penguin species, seven live in **Antarctic** seas such as the Southern Ocean, which lies between the Antarctic continent and the South Polar Front. This is where cold Antarctic water meets warmer subtropical water.

The best-known of all penguins is probably the Adèlie penguin. It is certainly the most-photographed and most-studied, and so has become most people's idea of what penguins look like. It is the active, smart little penguin in a "dinner jacket"—black back and white front—with white rings around its eyes. The Adèlie is the most widely distributed of the Antarctic penguins, breeding on rocky coastlines right around the continent, and on islands to the north. At about twelve pounds, it is not a big penguin. However, it will fiercely defend its territory from other penguins, or people.

The only other penguin that lives right around the Antarctic continent

◀ *The second-largest penguin is the emperor's cousin, the king penguin. It looks like a shorter, thinner version of the emperor, with a straighter, thicker bill, and brighter colors. It weighs from twenty-five to thirty-five pounds.*

is the emperor penguin, the largest of all penguins. Standing about three feet tall, it weighs up to 100 pounds, depending on how well it has eaten in recent months. All but two of the forty or so known colonies are on the sea ice that forms in autumn, so most emperor penguins probably never touch land during their entire lives.

Three more types of penguins—the gentoo, chinstrap, and macaroni—also nest on the Antarctic continent, but only on the peninsula, as well as islands farther north. The macaroni penguin is

▲ *Penguins often hitch rides on passing icebergs or ice floes. These times are for resting. To get up onto an iceberg like this one, the penguins swim at full speed, leap up to seven feet out of the water, and grip the surface of the ice with their very long toenails.*

the most numerous penguin on Earth. In the Southern Ocean, there are well over 10 million breeding pairs (over 20 million individual birds), plus an unknown but large number of nonbreeding birds. That's a lot of birds that need much **krill** and fish to eat.

The five-pound rockhopper penguin is the smallest of the Antarctic species, but it makes up for this by being the most **aggressive** of all the penguins.

4

The Largest Penguin

Emperor penguins are the largest penguins on Earth. The emperors have made many **adaptations** to keep themselves warm. They have large, rounded bodies. Their feet, flippers, head, and bill are all small when compared to the rest of the body. More than $3/4$ of their insulation is provided by their remarkable feathers. The feathers overlap like tiles on a roof to form a waterproof layer that is

▲   *Emperor penguins*

▲ *Seventy pounds of emperor penguin explodes out of the sea and up onto the sea ice. The emperor penguin is clearly the champion among diving birds.*

strong enough to protect them from the worst **blizzards**. A layer of fat under the skin completes the insulation and acts as a food reserve. At the beginning of winter, this fat layer is more than an inch thick.

Possibly the most important adaptation—and certainly the most amazing—is "huddling." Whenever the weather becomes too harsh, the birds pack tightly together. This halves the heat loss of all the birds except those at the outer edge of the huddle, and ensures that their food reserves will last much longer. Every penguin takes its turn acting as a windbreaker on the cold side before shuffling around to the sheltered side to join the huddle again.

The Life Cycle of an Emperor

Most birds look after their chicks until they are about adult size. In Antarctica, there simply isn't time for that. The summer is too short, so both Adèlie and emperor penguin juveniles finish their growing in the pack ice at a time when food is still plentiful.

In smaller penguin species, the chicks can look after themselves two months after hatching, so the whole cycle can be squeezed into the short, Antarctic summer.

A chick waves its head from side to side, begging for food. ▶

13

▲ *Here is an aerial view of Antarctica's second-largest emperor penguin colony at Cape Washington, Ross Sea.*

◄ *An emperor chick peers out from its safe home on its parent's feet, under the same fold of skin that protects the egg from the winter cold.*

14

Emperor chicks grow into much larger birds and need five months before they can face the world alone. The only way that youngsters can leave the colony in midsummer is for the parents to begin the breeding cycle much earlier than other penguins—in the previous autumn!

In autumn, the emperors assemble at their **colonies** on the sea ice close to shore. Here they court and **mate**. As winter deepens, the female lays her single egg and hands it over to the male. With his bill, he rolls it carefully up onto his feet. Here it is warmed against a patch of bare skin, and protected by a fold of belly skin that rolls down to cover it completely. The female now heads for the sea. By this time she has lost a quarter of her body weight and needs to fatten up before the chick hatches.

For the next two months, the male balances the egg on his feet through the dark Antarctic winter. Blizzards batter him, and temperatures drop as low as seventy-six degrees below zero **Fahrenheit**. He huddles with other males, day after day... after day. During winter, the male does not eat for three to four months; this is a longer fast than any other bird can endure.

The female returns about the time the egg hatches. Then the male wanders off, thin and scruffy, to look for open water and a meal! The female feeds the chick for three weeks until the male

Huddling is the emperor penguins' highly effective defense against Antarctic blizzards. A big huddle can include up to 6,000 birds. Huddles are remarkable acts of peaceful cooperation against a common enemy—the cold.

returns. From then on, the pair runs a shuttle service to deliver food to the chick.

By midsummer, the chick, now four to five months old, gets its last meal from its parents. The youngster now has to make its own way in the world, though it doesn't yet look old enough— large patches of down still cling to its waterproof feathers, and it weighs only twenty to thirty pounds, or half the adult weight.

The first year is tough, and many young penguins die. The ones that *do* **survive** return to the colony. There they breed in four to six years. Of those reaching adulthood, most will live for twenty to thirty years, and some will reach fifty years of age!

6

Adèlie Penguins

The Adèlie penguin is the best-known penguin. It is the funny, smart little "gentleman" in a black-and-white dinner suit, or perhaps a "nun" in her convent attire. It is the penguin most people picture when they think of penguins. The "surprised" white ring around its eyes adds to its appeal.

NOTES

The Adèlie penguin can be funny at times. These penguins yell and fight, squabble and steal, push and shove... but they also look after their mates, eggs, and chicks with total dedication. And they manage to survive some of the worst weather in the world.

Adèlie and emperor penguins are the only two penguin species that live right around the Antarctic continent. The Adèlie is by far the more common type of the two. Its stocky body weighs anywhere between eight and eighteen pounds. These penguins dive deep in search of krill and small fish. They are also strong swimmers.

Penguin parents recognize and feed only their own chicks. Here, a large Adèlie chick begs for food. Mealtime for chicks always means seafood—an oily mess of fish, krill, or whatever else the parent has caught on its feeding trip. The food is brought back in the parent's stomach, and then forced up (regurgitated) into the chick's mouth. It may not sound very tasty to us, but penguin chicks love it!

Each spring, these tough little penguins head south toward the Antarctic coastline, and the colony of their birth. Their colonies are on rocky, ice-free beaches in areas where the sea ice breaks up during summer. As a result, the penguins don't have to travel too far in order to feed.

The male arrives first, often at the exact nest site he had the year before. Hopefully his mate from last year will turn up soon. If she doesn't, he will look for a new partner. Two eggs are laid in a nest of small stones, and the parents take turns looking after the eggs, and then feeding the chicks.

Adèlie chicks grow fast. Seven to eight weeks after hatching, the youngsters molt into their waterproof feathers and head out to sea independently. They are not fully grown when they do this; they will finish their growth in the pack ice.

The chicks grow faster than any other penguin chicks. They have to, because soon the sea will start to freeze. By the time that happens, they will need to have grown their waterproof feathers and be in the pack ice, where they will spend winter. Every summer is a race against time.

▲   *This juvenile Adèlie penguin, seen here stretching, still has down attached to its waterproof plumage.*

◄   *Adèlie penguins nest on rocky, ice-free beaches in colonies around the Antarctic continent, and islands to the north. Colonies range in size from 100 to 250,000 pairs of penguins. Because the sites are exposed to sun and wind, snow does not bury them.*

Penguins in Warmer Seas

North of Antarctic seas in the Southern Ocean, we meet the remaining ten penguin species, as well as some we've met earlier. Two species of crested penguins, macaroni and rockhopper penguins, are very common in both Antarctic and warmer sub-Antarctic seas.

With their numbers pegged at well over 30 million, macaroni penguins are among the most common of all penguin species.

The six crested penguin species live in many different **habitats**, but all look very much alike, with their wild, tufted eyebrows of yellow feathers, short, stout bodies, and thick beaks. In warmer seas, we meet the other four crested penguin species: the royal, erect-crested, Snares crested, and Fiordland crested penguins. These species breed only in specific areas in the New

▲ *This Snares crested penguin seems to be posing for a portrait!*

Zealand region. The Snares crested penguin lives only on the tiny Snares Islands, to the south of New Zealand. Here it sometimes roosts and nests in low trees.

The royal penguin is larger than the macaroni penguin. It has a white face and throat, and it nests only on Macquarie Island, south of New Zealand.

The ringed penguins are the least "Antarctic" penguins. Three of the four species, Peruvian, Magellanic, and Galapagos penguins, live

▲ *The rockhopper penguin is one of the smallest penguins, but also one of the noisiest and most aggressive. Only about a foot high, it will attack anyone or anything it views as a threat. As its name implies, it is a "rockhopper," good at jumping from boulder to boulder, or hopping up steep, rocky slopes with both feet side by side. Like all crested penguins, the rockhopper's crest lies flat against its head in the water; it springs up only when the bird dries off.*

around the coasts of South America. The fourth, the African penguin, lives in South Africa. The Galapagos penguin lives at the equator on the Galapagos Islands.

The last two species are the yellow-eyed and blue penguins.

The Smallest Penguin

The world's smallest penguin is the blue penguin, also called the little or fairy penguin. It stands about twelve inches tall and weighs about two pounds. It has a blue-gray back and white front, and it is the only penguin that does not have colors or crests on its head. The blue penguin lives around New Zealand and

In the chicks' first three weeks of life, one parent guards the chicks constantly while the other is out at sea, feeding. ▼

NOTES

I don't often see little penguins ashore (unless I go looking for them after dark), but almost every time I go to sea near my home in New Zealand, I see these small, likeable penguins. Usually they are alone, but sometimes I see them in small groups. As our boat approaches, they usually dive and swim away underwater, but one penguin was different. It swam around the yacht I was on for over an hour.

Blue penguins nest in caves, crevices, burrows, or other sheltered places on the shore. ▶

southern Australia. Unlike most other penguin species, blue penguins usually stay in the same area year-round, even after the breeding season is over.

These small, stout penguins spend their days at sea hunting for food. They eat small schooling fish, squid, krill, sea horses, octopuses, and other small prey that they swallow whole. Dives last less than thirty seconds and are usually less than seventy feet in depth. When they have to, though, they can dive up to 200 feet.

For much of the year, blue penguins live in pairs in loose colonies along the coastline. They make their homes in burrows, caves, and other sheltered places. They leave before dawn and return after dark.

Males and females share in building the nest, looking after the eggs, and raising the chicks. The eggs take five weeks to hatch. Eight weeks after hatching, the chicks are ready to head out to sea by themselves.

If there's plenty of food in the sea, blue penguins often raise a second family—and sometimes even a third—during a single breeding season. Most blue penguins live for five to ten years, and sometimes up to twenty-five years.

9

The Yellow-Eyed Penguin

"Hoiho," the Noise Shouter

The yellow-eyed penguin cannot be confused with any other penguin. Its yellow eyes and headband are distinctive. This penguin's **Maori** name is *Hoiho*, which means "noise shouter." Its high-pitched, ear-piercing call is used when greeting another bird, courting, claiming territory, or whenever it feels threatened. The Hoiho may be a noisy bird, but it is also very shy, so it is heard more often than it is seen.

▲ *Yellow-eyed penguin*

Standing twenty-four to twenty-seven inches tall and weighing anywhere between eleven and eighteen pounds, the yellow-eyed penguin is so different from all other penguins that scientists put it in a group by itself.

Many penguins nest in large, noisy colonies, but the Hoiho is different. It nests in coastal forests and scrub, sometimes more than half a mile from the sea. The Hoiho needs space and privacy. Each pair chooses a nest site where they cannot be seen by any other penguins. Apart from the young birds that wander widely, the Hoiho stays near home year-round.

▲ *Yellow-eyed penguins come ashore through slippery bull kelp. Knowing that this is one of the world's rarest penguins, seeing this many is a wonderful sight.*

Two eggs are laid in spring, and often both chicks are successfully reared, which is unusual among penguins. For the first six weeks, one parent guards the chicks while the other parent goes fishing. The chicks grow rapidly, and by the time they are six weeks old, both parents must go fishing to feed them. At fifteen weeks, the chicks are ready to go to sea. Hoiho can live to be over twenty years old. They usually stay with the same partner for life.

10

The Circle of Life

Most penguins breed in colonies. Some of these are huge, with up to a million pairs. Penguins return to the same breeding areas every year, and often to the same nest site. Their unions often last for many years. In some species, the pairs stay together through the year. Normally, pairs meet up again when both birds arrive at the breeding area at the end of winter. If their mate does not arrive in time, they will choose another mate.

Most species lay one or two eggs, but some lay up to four. Males and females share all the tasks: building the nest, keeping the eggs warm, and guarding and feeding the chicks. The parents bring back food in their stomachs, feeding the chicks by **regurgitating** the food into their mouths. In most species, older chicks gather in **crèches** for protection from both predators and the weather.

◀ *An Adèlie penguin checks its precious eggs.*

Skuas prey on Adèlie penguin chicks and eggs at the edge of the colony. They sometimes work in pairs—one bird distracts the penguin on the nest, while the other swoops in to steal the egg or chick. When the chicks get to this size, they are mostly safe from skuas. ▶

Those penguins that *do* survive the first few years can look forward to a long life. Like most seabirds, penguins are normally long-lived. They take anywhere from three to eight years before they are ready to breed—sometimes even longer. Their average lifespan is between ten and twenty years—sometimes more. Of those reaching adulthood, most emperor penguins live for up to thirty years. Some even reach fifty years of age!

Penguins face many dangers. Starvation is probably the most crucial threat; it kills many penguins when they cannot find enough food at sea. El Niño weather patterns warm the seas in some years, reducing food levels. Then there are the predators. In the sea, these are leopard seals, sea lions, fur seals, orcas, and sharks. On land, penguin eggs and chicks are in danger from natural predators, such as **skuas**, giant petrels, eagles, snakes, and lizards, as well as introduced predators.

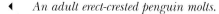
An adult erect-crested penguin molts.

All penguins need to replace their feathers each year. Adults usually do this after the breeding season. Molting takes about three weeks. As penguins lose their waterproof feathers during molting, they cannot go to sea to feed, so they stand around, fasting and looking miserable. Penguins are very vulnerable to predators or human disturbance when they are molting.

Penguin chicks are kept warm by a thick coat of downy feathers that allows them to be independent of their parents. Since this down is not waterproof, the chicks cannot go to sea until their feathers have grown.

As soon as penguin chicks grow their waterproof feathers, they head out to sea to fend for themselves. This is a difficult and dangerous time for the youngsters. They must quickly learn how to find and catch their own food, as well as avoid predators. Many die during their first few months, and less than half survive into adulthood.

11

Penguins and People

Over the past 200 years, humans have killed penguins by the millions. Some penguins were eaten, some were killed for their feathers, and others were simply boiled for their oil. Penguin eggs were taken by the tens of millions, and are still being taken by tens of thousands. On some islands, penguins are still killed for their feathers, oil, and skins. Some fishermen still use penguin meat for bait.

It's not just what we do intentionally, but also what we do by accident that matters. Penguins **evolved** on predator-free islands. When predators are introduced, they threaten most

NOTES

Writing this chapter makes me sad.

What cheers me up is knowing that you are reading it, and that some of you care enough about penguins and our planet to make a real difference. So, what can you do? Learn as much as you can about penguins and the other wonderful animals, plants, and places on our planet. Learn what the problems are, and then choose something you can do that will make a difference.

birds, especially ones that cannot fly. Dogs, cats, pigs, ferrets, and rats all kill penguins, sometimes in large numbers. Farming, logging, and other human activities destroy the breeding places of some penguins. If people catch too many of the fish that penguins eat, it becomes more difficult for them to feed.

Oil spills, garbage dumped into the sea, DDT (a harmful pesticide), fishing nets, and other kinds of **pollution** all harm the penguin's fragile way of life.

Oil spills are a constant threat to African penguins living along one of the world's main shipping routes, around South Africa. There have already been some serious spills. After one oil spill, volunteers from around the world raced to help clean up and care for tens of

◀ *A sign warns motorists to watch out for penguins going to and from their nests. The message is written in Maori as well as English.*

Rolled penguin skins discovered in a cave on the sub-Antarctic Antipodes Islands are remnants of the days of sealing. Penguin skins were used to make caps, slippers, hand warmers, and purses. Their feathers were used to decorate clothing and also as mattress stuffing. ▶

thousands of penguins. But each year, more and bigger ships travel along this coastline. What will happen the next time there is an oil spill? And the time after that?

Global warming also has an adverse affect on penguins. Antarctic penguins feed almost entirely on krill, and big populations of krill are only produced during "super winters" in Antarctica. These winters are much colder than normal, which lets baby krill survive in huge numbers. Global warming has already reduced krill populations, badly affecting the nesting success of Antarctic penguins.

THE DOMINIE WORLD OF
OCEAN LIFE

A N T A R C T I C A

Glossary

Adaptations:	Gradual physical changes or adjustments that enable an animal to survive in its environment, even under severe conditions
Aggressive:	Showing a tendency to attack or do harm to others
Antarctic:	Relating to the South Pole or the area surrounding it
Antarctica:	An uninhabited continent surrounding the South Pole
Blizzards:	Severe snowstorms with powerful winds
Camouflage:	A device used by some animals to blend into their surroundings in order to avoid being seen by predators or prey
Colonies:	Groups of animals of the same kind that live together and are dependent on one another
Crèches:	Penguin nurseries where young chicks gather for protection
Equator:	An imaginary line circling the Earth and dividing the planet into the northern and southern hemispheres
Evolve:	To undergo gradual physical changes over time
Fahrenheit:	A temperature scale on which water normally freezes at 32 degrees
Habitats:	Areas where animals and plants live and grow
Insulation:	Something that prevents or reduces the loss of warmth
Krill:	A very small shrimp-like marine animal that is a primary source of food for penguins, whales, and many other inhabitants of Antarctica
Maori:	The language spoken by some Polynesian people who are native to New Zealand
Mate (v):	To join with another animal in order to produce offspring
Molt:	To periodically shed feathers, hair, or skin and replace what is lost with new growth
Pollution:	Contamination
Predator:	An animal that hunts, catches, and eats other animals
Propel:	To move something forward
Regurgitate:	An animal's ability to bring up incompletely digested food from its stomach to feed to its young
Skuas:	A wide-ranging group of seabirds
Southern Hemisphere:	The half of the Earth located south of the equator
Species:	Types of animals that have some physical characteristics in common
Streamlined:	Designed to move very quickly and gracefully
Survive:	To stay alive and thrive